DEPORTED
ALIENS

Rob Staeger

THE CHANGING
Face of North America:
IMMIGRATION SINCE 1965

DEPORTED ALIENS

Rob Staeger

MASON CREST PUBLISHERS
PHILADELPHIA

Produced by OTTN Publishing, Stockton, New Jersey

Mason Crest Publishers
370 Reed Road
Broomall, PA 19008
www.masoncrest.com

First printing

1 3 5 7 9 8 6 4 2

Library of Congress Cataloging-in-Publication Data

Staeger, Rob.
  Deported aliens / Rob Staeger.
      p. cm. — (The changing face of North America)
Summary: An overview of immigration of illegal aliens to the United States and Canada since the 1960s, as a result
of changes in immigration law.
Includes bibliographical references and index.
  ISBN 1-59084-686-9
  1. Illegal aliens—United States. 2. United States—Emigration and immigration—Government policy. 3. Illegal
aliens—Canada. 4. Canada—Emigration and immigration—Government policy. [1. Illegal aliens.] I. Title. II. Series.
  JV6483. S63 2004
  325.73—dc22
                                                                    2003018811

THE **CHANGING**
Face of North America:
IMMIGRATION SINCE 1965

CONTENTS

INTRODUCTION

THE CHANGING FACE OF AMERICA

By Senator Edward M. Kennedy

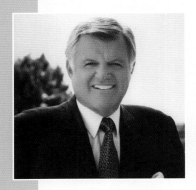

America is proud of its heritage and history as a nation of immigrants, and my own family is an example. All eight of my great-grandparents were immigrants who left Ireland a century and a half ago, when that land was devastated by the massive famine caused by the potato blight. When I was a young boy, my grandfather used to take me down to the docks in Boston and regale me with stories about the Great Famine and the waves of Irish immigrants who came to America seeking a better life. He talked of how the Irish left their marks in Boston and across the nation, enduring many hardships and harsh discrimination, but also building the railroads, digging the canals, settling the West, and filling the factories of a growing America. According to one well-known saying of the time, "under every railroad tie, an Irishman is buried."

America was the promised land for them, as it has been for so many other immigrants who have found shelter, hope, opportunity, and freedom. Immigrants have always been an indispensable part of our nation. They have contributed immensely to our communities, created new jobs and whole new industries, served in our armed forces, and helped make America the continuing land of promise that it is today.

The inspiring poem by Emma Lazarus, inscribed on the pedestal of the Statue of Liberty in New York Harbor, is America's welcome to all immigrants:

Give me your tired, your poor,
Your huddled masses yearning to breathe free,
The wretched refuse of your teeming shore,
Send these, the homeless, tempest-tossed, to me:
I lift my lamp beside the golden door.

The period since September 11, 2001, has been particularly challenging for immigrants. Since the horrifying terrorist attacks, there has been a resurgence of anti-immigrant attitudes and behavior. We all agree that our borders must be safe and secure. Yet, at the same time, we must safeguard the entry of the millions of persons who come to the United States legally each year as immigrants, visitors, scholars, students, and workers. The "golden door" must stay open. We must recognize that immigration is not the problem—terrorism is. We must identify and isolate the terrorists, and not isolate America.

One of my most important responsibilities in the Senate is the preservation of basic rights and basic fairness in the application of our immigration laws, so that new generations of immigrants in our own time and for all time will have the same opportunity that my great-grandparents had when they arrived in America.

Immigration is beneficial for the United States and for countries throughout the world. It is no coincidence that two hundred years ago, our nations' founders chose *E Pluribus Unum*—"out of many, one"—as America's motto. These words, chosen by Benjamin Franklin, John Adams, and Thomas Jefferson, refer to the ideal that separate colonies can be transformed into one united nation. Today, this ideal has come to apply to individuals as well. Our diversity is our strength. We are a nation of immigrants, and we always will be.

Foreword

The Changing Face of the United States

Marian L. Smith, historian
U.S. Immigration and Naturalization Service

Americans commonly assume that immigration today is very different than immigration of the past. The immigrants themselves appear to be unlike immigrants of earlier eras. Their language, their dress, their food, and their ways seem strange. At times people fear too many of these new immigrants will destroy the America they know. But has anything really changed? Do new immigrants have any different effect on America than old immigrants a century ago? Is the American fear of too much immigration a new development? Do immigrants really change America more than America changes the immigrants? The very subject of immigration raises many questions.

In the United States, immigration is more than a chapter in a history book. It is a continuous thread that links the present moment to the first settlers on North American shores. From the first colonists' arrival until today, immigrants have been met by Americans who both welcomed and feared them. Immigrant contributions were always welcome—on the farm, in the fields, and in the factories. Welcoming the poor, the persecuted, and the "huddled masses" became an American principle. Beginning with the original Pilgrims' flight from religious persecution in the 1600s, through the Irish migration to escape starvation in the 1800s, to the relocation of Central Americans seeking refuge from civil wars in the 1980s and 1990s, the United States has considered itself a haven for the destitute and the oppressed.

But there was also concern that immigrants would not adopt American ways, habits, or language. Too many immigrants might overwhelm America. If so, the dream of the Founding Fathers for United States government and society would be destroyed. For this reason, throughout American history some have argued that limiting or ending immigration is our patriotic duty. Benjamin Franklin feared there were so many German immigrants in Pennsylvania the Colonial Legislature would begin speaking German. "Progressive" leaders of the early 1900s feared that immigrants who could not read and understand the English language were not only exploited by "big business," but also served as the foundation for "machine politics" that undermined the U.S. Constitution. This theme continues today, usually voiced by those who bear no malice toward immigrants but who want to preserve American ideals.

Have immigrants changed? In colonial days, when most colonists were of English descent, they considered Germans, Swiss, and French immigrants as different. They were not "one of us" because they spoke a different language. Generations later, Americans of German or French descent viewed Polish, Italian, and Russian immigrants as strange. They were not "like us" because they had a different religion, or because they did not come from a tradition of constitutional government. Recently, Americans of Polish or Italian descent have seen Nicaraguan, Pakistani, or Vietnamese immigrants as too different to be included. It has long been said of American immigration that the latest ones to arrive usually want to close the door behind them.

It is important to remember that fear of individual immigrant groups seldom lasted, and always lessened. Benjamin Franklin's anxiety over German immigrants disappeared after those immigrants' sons and daughters helped the nation gain independence in the Revolutionary War. The Irish of the mid-1800s were among the most hated immigrants, but today we all wear green on St. Patrick's Day. While a century ago it was feared that Italian and other Catholic immigrants would vote as directed by the Pope, today that controversy is only a vague memory. Unfortunately, some ethnic groups continue their efforts to earn acceptance. The African

Americans' struggle continues, and some Asian Americans, whose families have been in America for generations, are the victims of current anti-immigrant sentiment.

Time changes both immigrants and America. Each wave of new immigrants, with their strange language and habits, eventually grows old and passes away. Their American-born children speak English. The immigrants' grandchildren are completely American. The strange foods of their ancestors—spaghetti, baklava, hummus, or tofu—become common in any American restaurant or grocery store. Much of what the immigrants brought to these shores is lost, principally their language. And what is gained becomes as American as St. Patrick's Day, Hanukkah, or Cinco de Mayo, and we forget that it was once something foreign.

Recent immigrants are all around us. They come from every corner of the earth to join in the American Dream. They will continue to help make the American Dream a reality, just as all the immigrants who came before them have done.

FOREWORD

THE CHANGING FACE OF CANADA

Peter A. Hammerschmidt
First Secretary, Permanent Mission of Canada to the United Nations

Throughout Canada's history, immigration has shaped and defined the very character of Canadian society. The migration of peoples from every part of the world into Canada has profoundly changed the way we look, speak, eat, and live. Through close and distant relatives who left their lands in search of a better life, all Canadians have links to immigrant pasts. We are a nation built by and of immigrants.

Two parallel forces have shaped the history of Canadian immigration. The enormous diversity of Canada's immigrant population is the most obvious. In the beginning came the enterprising settlers of the "New World," the French and English colonists. Soon after came the Scottish, Irish, and Northern and Central European farmers of the 1700s and 1800s. As the country expanded westward during the mid-1800s, migrant workers began arriving from China, Japan, and other Asian countries. And the turbulent twentieth century brought an even greater variety of immigrants to Canada, from the Caribbean, Africa, India, and Southeast Asia.

So while English- and French-Canadians are the largest ethnic groups in the country today, neither group alone represents a majority of the population. A large and vibrant multicultural mix makes up the rest, particularly in Canada's major cities. Toronto, Vancouver, and Montreal alone are home to people from over 200 ethnic groups!

Less obvious but equally important in the evolution of Canadian immigration has been hope. The promise of a better life lured Europeans and Americans seeking cheap (sometimes even free) farmland. Thousands of Scots and Irish arrived to escape grinding poverty and starvation. Others came for freedom, to escape religious and political persecution. Canada has long been a haven to the world's dispossessed and disenfranchised—Dutch and German farmers cast out for their religious beliefs, black slaves fleeing the United States, and political refugees of despotic regimes in Europe, Africa, Asia, and South America.

The two forces of diversity and hope, so central to Canada's past, also shaped the modern era of Canadian immigration. Following the Second World War, Canada drew heavily on these influences to forge trailblazing immigration initiatives.

The catalyst for change was the adoption of the Canadian Bill of Rights in 1960. Recognizing its growing diversity and Canadians' changing attitudes towards racism, the government passed a federal statute barring discrimination on the grounds of race, national origin, color, religion, or sex. Effectively rejecting the discriminatory elements in Canadian immigration policy, the Bill of Rights forced the introduction of a new policy in 1962. The focus of immigration abruptly switched from national origin to the individual's potential contribution to Canadian society. The door to Canada was now open to every corner of the world.

Welcoming those seeking new hopes in a new land has also been a feature of Canadian immigration in the modern era. The focus on economic immigration has increased along with Canada's steadily growing economy, but political immigration has also been encouraged. Since 1945, Canada has admitted tens of thousands of displaced persons, including Jewish Holocaust survivors, victims of Soviet crackdowns in Hungary and Czechoslovakia, and refugees from political upheaval in Uganda, Chile, and Vietnam.

Prior to 1978, however, these political refugees were admitted as an exception to normal immigration procedures. That year, Canada revamped its refugee policy with a new Immigration Act that explicitly affirmed Canada's commitment to the resettlement of refugees from oppression. Today, the admission of refugees remains a central part of Canadian immigration law and regulations.

Amendments to economic and political immigration policy continued during the 1980s and 1990s, refining further the bold steps taken during the modern era. Together, these initiatives have turned Canada into one of the world's few truly multicultural states.

Unlike the process of assimilation into a "melting pot" of cultures, immigrants to Canada are more likely to retain their cultural identity, beliefs, and practices. This is the source of some of Canada's greatest strengths as a society. And as a truly multicultural nation, diversity is not seen as a threat to Canadian identity. Quite the contrary—diversity *is* Canadian identity.

1 WHAT IS DEPORTATION?

D iego Ramirez, a Mexican man in his 20s, waited by the banks of the Rio Grande. He was alone. Far upriver, he could hear people milling around, but he kept his distance from them, knowing that his chances were better moving alone. Night would come soon, and Diego planned to cross the river into the United States. In the distance, he saw a U.S. Border Patrol agent scanning the river with his binoculars.

Night fell, but Diego still waited for the right time. He carefully undressed, tucking his blue jeans and wallet in a large plastic bag. A New York Mets baseball cap and a green T-shirt with a "Nike—Just do it" logo went into another. He sealed the bags and listened. Upriver, the chattering had stopped. All was silent.

He thought he heard a small splash. It sounded like the *plip-plop* of someone losing his footing in the water. Then the shouting started. Diego had been waiting for it. With the Border Patrol rounding up the upriver crowd, he planned to move unnoticed during the commotion. Diego waded into the river in just his sneakers and his underwear. He crossed in silence. The chest-deep current was strong, but he pushed through.

On the Texas side, he opened his Ziploc bags and dressed quickly into the dry clothes. He stuffed the bags in his pockets

◀A Mexican man wades through the sewage-filled New River to cross the border into Calexico, California. Every year thousands of migrants illegally enter the United States by walking across the border or passing undetected through ports of entry. Many who make it into the country are deported after immigration agencies track them down.

and hurried off, keeping low to the ground. The next destination was El Paso, where he had the name of a coyote (smuggler) who could get him a job.

Meanwhile, Border Patrol Agent Neil Hightower had been waiting for Diego to move while his fellow guards were dealing with the crowd of entrants. Hightower stayed in hiding, watching the river with night-vision binoculars. The air patrol had spotted Diego that afternoon, and Hightower had decided to wait him out.

He kept his eye on Diego as he drifted downriver. Hightower drove his SUV to where Diego had come ashore. The migrant had already run off but the agent had no trouble following his path. Every day the agents smoothed the dirt by the river; all Hightower had to do was follow the distinct set of wet footprints.

He caught up with Diego about a mile away. The agent handcuffed him and drove him back to the station. There Hightower asked Diego how he got over the border, although he already knew the answer. He also asked whom Diego had planned to see next, and had a pretty good idea of that answer, too. It could have been any of the coyotes familiar to Hightower who operate out of El Paso, though Diego refused to name which one. Then the migrant was fingerprinted and photographed. A computer analyzed his prints, and found a match. Apparently, Diego had tried to cross three times before.

Diego was eventually put in a holding cell with the group that had attempted to cross upriver. The next morning, they would all be driven back to the border. Most of them would probably try again in the near future. Still, the agents had dealt with the problem as best they could. To formally deport every illegal entrant would clog the court system. Plus, where would they stay while they waited for hearings? There were no jails big enough to hold them all.

* * *

Three years ago, Liam had come to the United States from Ireland on a visitor's visa. Since then, he'd done anything he could to make a buck. He worked for a landscaping company in the spring and summer. When the weather turned cooler, he washed dishes and bussed tables at a restaurant. The kitchen was full of Irish immigrants like him. All the work was temporary, and everyone was paid in cash.

Liam was scrubbing his way through a sink of dirty dishes when two men in suits walked into the kitchen. "We're from the Bureau of Immigration and Customs Enforcement," one said. "Where's your manager?"

A waitress pointed to the kitchen office door. One of the officers knocked and went in. The other looked at the kitchen staff. "I'm going to need to see some ID," he said. It was then Liam knew for sure his plans had changed. He was going to be deported.

Deportation and Its Limitations

The above examples are composite characters and situations. While Diego, Liam, Agent Hightower, and the two officers are fictional, the details of their situations and the procedures they undergo are real, and were drawn from immigration law and Border Patrol protocol.

Deportation is the formal removal of an alien from a country. It is one of the ways that the U.S. and Canadian governments control immigration. Some foreigners legally arrive into the county and then break certain laws. Others break laws by entering illegally. Others enter legally, but stay after they have been ordered to leave. All these people can potentially be deported.

In reality, only some of these people will be deported. Immigration agents face limitations on whom they can find and who escapes their notice. But when the government tries to remove aliens, it must do so fairly. People who face possible deportation are guaranteed a fair and proper hearing as long as they do not waive that right.

2 THE CHALLENGE OF IMMIGRATION ENFORCEMENT

Spanning 4,000 miles, the northern border between the United States and Canada is one of the longest in the world. The United States shares another 2,000 miles of border with Mexico. Along these borders, there are over 300 land-based ports of entry. Separate from the borders are 12,383 miles of coastline, as well as commercial airports through which people enter the United States. Considering these great dimensions, it's easy to see how large and complicated the task of controlling immigration is.

The United States allows 800,000 to 1 million people to immigrate legally each year. Millions more come to the United States to travel. Like U.S. citizens and permanent residents, visitors must follow certain rules of conduct. Specific rules also apply to those who come over on visas. A visa is an official authorization that allows a person to enter the country at a port, which is permitted only by an immigration/customs inspector. Even if an alien has a visa, the individual may not enter the country if the inspector concludes that he or she is not eligible to be admitted.

The conditions that visa holders are obligated to meet are clearly spelled out. For example, if someone from India comes to the United States on a student visa, he or she must be enrolled in a college and be taking a full load of classes each semester (although this requirement doesn't apply to students

◀ A reporter points out an error in the visa application of Hani Hanjour, one of the terrorists involved in the attacks of September 11, 2001. Some deportable aliens enter the United States with fraudulent visas; others enter with legitimate documents but fail to meet the specific conditions of their visa while they are living in the country.

commuting from Canada or Mexico). Other kinds of people can receive visas besides students. They include workers, athletes, and entertainers, all of whom must meet the specific conditions of their visa category and not break certain rules, or face removal from the country.

Beyond breaking the rules after entering a country, there are others reasons people can be deported. Some people come to the United States without going through the proper legal channels. These individuals are called undocumented, or illegal, immigrants.

A Civil Matter

Deportation is not a criminal punishment. While it may be the legal result of a criminal act, deportation is a civil matter. Whatever the crime, and whoever the criminal, it is not possible to be sentenced to be deported. Deportation hearings are separate from criminal trials, and often begin only after the criminal case has been resolved.

Aliens, including those with lawful permanent resident status, are the only candidates for deportation. The law prohibits the deportation of U.S. citizens (except under very rare circumstances), as well as select groups of aliens. This latter group includes official representatives of foreign governments— ambassadors, diplomats, consular officers, and their families. Employees of the United Nations also are immune from being deported.

Other aliens may mistakenly think they are immune from deportation, particularly parents of U.S. citizens. Although their children are born in the United States, which automatically makes them citizens, as foreign nationals they do not enjoy the same protection.

There are many other complex regulations governing deportation, but before examining these and related issues, it is important to become familiar with North American immigration policy and how it has changed throughout history.

A Short History of U.S. Immigration

Immigration to the United States has been characterized by openness punctuated by periods of restriction. During the 17th, 18th, and 19th centuries, immigration was essentially open without restriction, and, at times, immigrants were even recruited to come to America. Between 1783 and 1820, approximately 250,000 immigrants arrived at U.S. shores. Between 1841 and 1860, more than 4 million immigrants came; most were from England, Ireland, and Germany.

Historically, race and ethnicity have played a role in legislation to restrict immigration. The Chinese Exclusion Act of 1882, which was not repealed until 1943, specifically prevented Chinese people from becoming U.S. citizens and did not

A satirical cartoon entitled "A Statue for Our Harbor," printed in an 1881 issue of the San Francisco–based magazine *The Wasp*, represents an anti-immigration perspective that persisted throughout much of U.S. history. The cartoon attributes social problems like immorality, disease, filth, and the ruin of "white labor" to Chinese immigrants. It appeared a year before Congress passed the Chinese Exclusion Act of 1882, which prohibited the Chinese from immigrating to the United States.

A STATUE FOR *OUR* HARBOR.

Immigrants stand with their luggage beneath a terminal at New York City's Ellis Island, 1905. More than one million immigrants a year—primarily from western European countries—arrived into the United States in the early 20th century.

allow Chinese laborers to immigrate for the next decade. An agreement with Japan in the early 1900s prevented most Japanese immigration to the United States.

Until the 1920s, no numerical restrictions on immigration existed in the United States, although health restrictions applied. The only other significant restrictions came in 1917, when passing a literacy test became a requirement for immigrants. Presidents Cleveland, Taft, and Wilson had vetoed similar measures earlier. In addition, in 1917 a prohibition was added to the law against the immigration of people from Asia (defined as the Asiatic barred zone). While a few of these prohibitions were lifted during World War II, they were not repealed until 1952, and even then Asians were only allowed in under very small annual quotas.

U.S. Immigration Policy from World War I to 1965

During World War I, the federal government required that all travelers to the United States obtain a visa at a U.S. consulate or diplomatic post abroad. As former State Department consular affairs officer C. D. Scully points out, by making that requirement permanent Congress, by 1924, established the framework of temporary, or non-immigrant visas (for study, work, or travel), and immigrant visas (for permanent residence). That framework remains in place today.

After World War I, cultural intolerance and bizarre racial theories led to new immigration restrictions. The House Judiciary Committee employed a eugenics consultant, Dr. Harry N. Laughlin, who asserted that certain races were inferior. Another leader of the eugenics movement, Madison Grant, argued that Jews, Italians, and others were inferior because of their supposedly different skull size.

The Immigration Act of 1924, preceded by the Temporary Quota Act of 1921, set new numerical limits on immigration based on "national origin." Taking effect in 1929, the 1924 act set annual quotas on immigrants that were specifically designed to keep out southern Europeans, such as Italians and Greeks. Generally no more than 100 people of the proscribed nationalities were permitted to immigrate.

While the new law was rigid, the U.S. Department of State's restrictive interpretation directed consular officers overseas to be even stricter in their application of the "public charge" provision. (A public charge is someone unable to support himself or his family.) As author Laura Fermi wrote, "In response to the new cry for restriction at the beginning of the [Great Depression] . . . the consuls were to interpret very strictly the clause prohibiting admission of aliens 'likely to become public charges; and to deny the visa to an applicant who in their opinion might become a public charge at any time.'"

In the early 1900s, more than one million immigrants a year came to the United States. In 1930—the first year of the national-origin quotas—approximately 241,700 immigrants were admitted. But under the State Department's strict interpretations, only 23,068 immigrants entered during 1933, the smallest total since 1831. Later these restrictions prevented many Jews in Germany and elsewhere in Europe from escaping what would become the Holocaust. At the height of the Holocaust in 1943, the United States admitted fewer than 6,000 refugees.

The Displaced Persons Act of 1948, the nation's first refugee law, allowed many refugees from World War II to settle in the United States. The law put into place policy changes that had already seen immigration rise from 38,119 in 1945 to 108,721 in 1946 (and later to 249,187 in 1950). One-third of those admitted between 1948 and 1951 were Poles, with ethnic Germans forming the second-largest group.

The 1952 Immigration and Nationality Act is best known for its restrictions against those who supported communism or anarchy. However, the bill's other provisions were quite restrictive and were passed over the veto of President Truman. The 1952 act retained the national-origin quota system for the Eastern Hemisphere. The Western Hemisphere continued to operate without a quota and relied on other qualitative factors to limit immigration. Moreover, during that time, the Mexican bracero program, from 1942 to 1964, allowed millions of Mexican agricultural workers to work temporarily in the United States.

The 1952 act set aside half of each national quota to be divided among three preference categories for relatives of U.S. citizens and permanent residents. The other half went to aliens with high education or exceptional abilities. These quotas applied only to those from the Eastern Hemisphere.

A Halt to the National-Origin Quotas

The Immigration and Nationality Act of 1965 became a landmark in immigration legislation by specifically striking the racially based national-origin quotas. It removed the barriers to Asian immigration, which later led to opportunities to immigrate for many Filipinos, Chinese, Koreans, and others. The Western Hemisphere was designated a ceiling of 120,000 immigrants but without a preference system or per country limits. Modifications made in 1978 ultimately combined the Western

When President Lyndon Johnson signed the Immigration Act of 1965, he inaugurated a new era of immigration. With the passage of the act, many previously excluded foreign groups were able to immigrate to the United States.

and Eastern Hemispheres into one preference system and one ceiling of 290,000.

The 1965 act built on the existing system—without the national-origin quotas—and gave somewhat more priority to family relationships. It did not completely overturn the existing system but rather carried forward essentially intact the family immigration categories from the 1959 amendments to the Immigration and Nationality Act. Even though the text of the law prior to 1965 indicated that half of the immigration slots were reserved for skilled employment immigration, in practice, Immigration and Naturalization Service (INS) statistics show that 86 percent of the visas issued between 1952 and 1965 went for family immigration.

A number of significant pieces of legislation since 1980 have shaped the current U.S. immigration system. First, the Refugee Act of 1980 removed refugees from the annual world limit and established that the president would set the number of refugees who could be admitted each year after consultations with Congress.

Second, the 1986 Immigration Reform and Control Act (IRCA) introduced sanctions against employers who "knowingly" hired undocumented immigrants (those here illegally). It also provided amnesty for many undocumented immigrants.

Third, the Immigration Act of 1990 increased legal immigration by 40 percent. In particular, the act significantly increased the number of employment-based immigrants (to 140,000), while also boosting family immigration.

Fourth, the 1996 Illegal Immigration Reform and Immigrant Responsibility Act (IIRAIRA) significantly tightened rules that permitted undocumented immigrants to convert to legal status and made other changes that tightened immigration law in areas such as political asylum and deportation.

Fifth, in response to the September 11, 2001, terrorist attacks, the USA PATRIOT Act and the Enhanced Border Security and Visa Entry Reform Act tightened rules on the granting of visas to individuals from certain countries and enhanced the federal government's monitoring and detention authority over foreign nationals in the United States.

New U.S. Immigration Agencies

In a dramatic reorganization of the federal government, the Homeland Security Act of 2002 abolished the Immigration and Naturalization Service and transferred its immigration service and enforcement functions from the Department of Justice into a new Department of Homeland Security. The Customs Service, the Coast Guard, and parts of other agencies were also transferred into the new department.

The Department of Homeland Security, with regards to immigration, is organized as follows: The Bureau of Customs and Border Protection (BCBP) contains Customs and Immigration inspectors, who check the documents of travelers to the United States at air, sea, and land ports of entry; and Border Patrol agents, the uniformed agents who seek to prevent unlawful entry along the southern and northern border. The new Bureau of Immigration and Customs Enforcement (BICE) employs investigators, who attempt to find undocumented immigrants inside the United States, and Detention and Removal officers, who detain and seek to deport such individuals. The new Bureau of Citizenship and Immigration Services (BCIS) is where people go, or correspond with, to become U.S. citizens or obtain permission to work or extend their stay in the United States.

Following the terrorist attacks of September 11, 2001, the Department of Justice adopted several measures that did not require new legislation to be passed by Congress. Some of these measures created controversy and raised concerns about civil liberties. For example, FBI and INS agents detained for months more than 1,000 foreign nationals of Middle Eastern descent and refused to release the names of the individuals. It is alleged that the Department of Justice adopted tactics that discouraged the detainees from obtaining legal assistance. The Department of Justice also began requiring foreign nationals from primarily Muslim nations to be fingerprinted and questioned by immigration officers upon entry or if they have been living in the United States. Those involved in the September 11 attacks were not immigrants—people who become permanent residents with a right to stay in the United States—but holders of temporary visas, primarily visitor or tourist visas.

Immigration to the United States Today

Today, the annual rate of legal immigration is lower than that at earlier periods in U.S. history. For example, from 1901 to 1910 approximately 10.4 immigrants per 1,000 U.S. residents came to the United States. Today, the annual rate is about 3.5 immigrants per 1,000 U.S. residents. While the percentage of foreign-born people in the U.S. population has risen above 11 percent, it remains lower than the 13 percent or higher that prevailed in the country from 1860 to 1930. Still, as has been the case previously in U.S. history, some people argue that even legal immigration should be lowered. These people maintain that immigrants take jobs native-born Americans could fill and that U.S. population growth, which immigration contributes to, harms the environment. In 1996 Congress voted against efforts to reduce legal immigration.

Most immigrants (800,000 to one million annually) enter the United States legally. But over the years the undocumented (illegal) portion of the population has increased to about 2.8 percent of the U.S. population—approximately 8 million people in all.

Today, the legal immigration system in the United States contains many rules, permitting only individuals who fit into certain categories to immigrate—and in many cases only after waiting anywhere from 1 to 10 years or more, depending on the demand in that category. The system, representing a compromise among family, employment, and human rights concerns, has the following elements:

A U.S. citizen may sponsor for immigration a spouse, parent, sibling, or minor or adult child.

A lawful permanent resident (green card holder) may sponsor only a spouse or child.

A foreign national may immigrate if he or she gains an employer sponsor.

An individual who can show that he or she has a "well-founded fear of persecution" may come to the country as a refugee—or be allowed to stay as an asylee (someone who receives asylum).

Beyond these categories, essentially the only other way to immigrate is to apply for and receive one of the "diversity" visas, which are granted annually by lottery to those from "underrepresented" countries.

In 1996 changes to the law prohibited nearly all incoming immigrants from being eligible for federal public benefits, such as welfare, during their first five years in the country. Refugees were mostly excluded from these changes. In addition, families who sponsor relatives must sign an affidavit of support showing they can financially take care of an immigrant who falls on hard times.

A Short History of Canadian Immigration

In the 1800s, immigration into Canada was largely unrestricted. Farmers and artisans from England and Ireland made up a significant portion of 19th-century immigrants. England's Parliament passed laws that facilitated and encouraged the voyage to North America, particularly for the poor.

After the United States barred Chinese railroad workers from settling in the country, Canada encouraged the immigration of Chinese laborers to assist in the building of Canadian railways. Responding to the racial views of the time, the Canadian Parliament began charging a "head tax" for Chinese and South Asian (Indian) immigrants in 1885. The fee of $50—later raised to $500—was well beyond the means of laborers making one or two dollars a day. Later, the government sought additional ways to prohibit Asians from entering the country. For example, it decided to require a "continuous journey," meaning that immigrants to Canada had to travel from their country on a boat that made an uninterrupted passage. For immigrants or asylum seekers from Asia this was nearly impossible.

As the 20th century progressed, concerns about race led to further restrictions on immigration to Canada. These restrictions particularly hurt Jewish and other refugees seeking to flee persecution in Europe. Government statistics indicate that Canada accepted no more than 5,000 Jewish refugees before and during the Holocaust.

After World War II, Canada, like the United States, began accepting thousands of Europeans displaced by the war. Canada's laws were modified to accept these war refugees, as well as Hungarians fleeing Communist authorities after the crushing of the 1956 Hungarian Revolution.

The Immigration Act of 1952 in Canada allowed for a "tap on, tap off" approach to immigration, granting administrative authorities the power to allow more immigrants into the country in good economic times, and fewer in times of recession. The shortcoming of such an approach is that there is little evidence immigrants harm a national economy and much evidence they contribute to economic growth, particularly in the growth of the labor force.

In 1966 the government of Prime Minister Lester Pearson introduced a policy statement stressing how immigrants were key to Canada's economic growth. With Canada's relatively small population base, it became clear that in the absence of newcomers, the country would not be able to grow. The policy was introduced four years after Parliament enacted important legislation that eliminated Canada's own version of racially based national-origin quotas.

In 1967 a new law established a points system that awarded entry to potential immigrants using criteria based primarily on an individual's age, language ability, skills, education, family relationships, and job prospects. The total points needed for entry of an immigrant is set by the Minister of Citizenship and Immigration Canada. The new law also established a category for humanitarian (refugee) entry.

The 1976 Immigration Act refined and expanded the possibility for entry under the points system, particularly for those seeking to sponsor family members. The act also expanded refugee and asylum law to comport with Canada's international obligations. The law established five basic categories for immigration into Canada: 1) family; 2) humanitarian; 3) independents (including skilled workers), who immigrate to Canada on their own; 4) assisted relatives; and 5) business immigrants (including investors, entrepreneurs, and the self-employed).

The new Immigration and Refugee Protection Act, which took effect June 28, 2002, made a series of modifications to existing Canadian immigration law. The act, and the regulations that followed, toughened rules on those seeking asylum and the process for removing people unlawfully in Canada.

The law modified the points system, adding greater flexibility for skilled immigrants and temporary workers to become permanent residents, and evaluating skilled workers on the weight of their transferable skills as well as those of their specific occupation. The legislation also made it easier for employers to have a labor shortage declared in an industry or sector, which would facilitate the entry of foreign workers in that industry or sector.

On family immigration, the act permitted parents to sponsor dependent children up to the age of 22 (previously 19 was the maximum age at which a child could be sponsored for immigration). The act also allowed partners in common-law arrangements, including same-sex partners, to be considered as family members for the purpose of immigration sponsorship. Along with these liberalizing measures, the act also included provisions to address perceived gaps in immigration-law enforcement.

Ports of Entry and Enforcement

For many aliens, pivotal events take place at a port of entry, the place where people are allowed to enter and exit the country. In some cases the conditions of an alien's status as an immigrant are established at a port of entry. In the United States there are more than 300 ports of entry where U.S.

citizens and people from other nations are inspected. These ports may be seaports, airports, and land entrances along the Canada and Mexico borders.

Generally, aliens must present a passport and a visa issued by a U.S. consulate. Some countries participate in the Visa Waiver Program, which allows foreign nationals to be admitted without a visa for up to 90 days. There are 27 participating countries in this program, including most of western Europe, as well as Australia, Brunei, Japan, New Zealand, Singapore, and Slovenia. Under a separate agreement, Canadians are also allowed in without a visa.

An immigration inspection officer allows most people to enter after examining their documents and speaking with them. Before visitors or immigrants pass through, the officer will explain the restrictions they must heed. Occasionally, he or she will stop someone from entering the country. This is called exclusion. Aliens can be excluded for criminal convictions, a lack of vaccinations, suspected terrorist activities, and other grounds.

If the alien seems excludable, he or she can be held for more questioning. In some cases, aliens are allowed in even though they are not formally admitted. This procedure is called parole. Inspectors parole aliens for a number of reasons. They may act out of a humanitarian concern or acknowledge a public benefit to the aliens' entry, for example.

In 1996, the Illegal Immigration Reform and Immigrant Responsibility Act permitted the use of "expedited removal" by immigration inspectors. Before expedited removal, aliens who did not leave voluntarily could only be removed or deported by a judge. This huge caseload during this period was expensive. It also meant that judges could not devote as much time to immigration cases that were less clear-cut.

Expedited removal allowed inspectors to immediately remove aliens who were deemed ineligible at a port. This process was quicker than holding a hearing for the individual; however, it raised concerns that asylum seekers could be turned back to a

A U.S. Customs inspector checks a woman's identity papers at the Paso del Norte port of entry in El Paso, Texas. After briefly asking a few important questions, inspectors will let most aliens through, although under special circumstances they may deny aliens entry.

country where they might be persecuted. To address these concerns, procedures were put in place that require those who have a "credible fear of persecution" to stay in the United States and pursue an asylum claim instead of being summarily removed.

An enforcement tool that some people consider even more effective than expedited removal is interdiction, the interception of migrants at sea by the U.S. Coast Guard. While expedited removal keeps certain people out of the country before they are admitted, interdiction keeps people from even reaching U.S. shores. As at a port of entry, aliens intercepted at sea can apply for asylum after proving a credible fear of persecution. All other migrants are towed back to their homeport by the Coast Guard.

3 UNDOCUMENTED IMMIGRANTS

Millions of undocumented immigrants live in the United States today. They avoid drawing attention to themselves to escape deportation, a fact that makes knowing the precise numbers of this group nearly impossible.

Researchers only can base their conclusions on estimates of the undocumented population. One of the best statistical sources to date is the report issued in January 2003 by the Immigration and Naturalization Service, *Estimates of the Unauthorized Immigrant Population Residing in the United States: 1990 to 2000.*

The report makes use of data from the 2000 U.S. Census and other sources. With this information, researchers have determined that 13.5 million foreign-born people moved to the United States during the 1990s. After subtracting the 8 million people who entered and remained in the country legally, researchers figured out that 5.5 million unauthorized aliens arrived during the decade. The INS then added a prior estimate of 1.5 million undocumented immigrants who were in the United States before 1990, which brought the decade's total of undocumented immigrants to 7 million people. In 2002 researchers estimated the total had grown to 8 million people.

On average, over the course of the decade the undocumented population grew by approximately 350,000 people each year.

◀ A Hispanic family walks down the street of an immigrant neighborhood of Los Angeles. Because undocumented immigrants typically aim to blend into the legal migrant community, government agencies face a great challenge in locating and deporting them.

This number includes new entrants as well as individuals removed from the population count, which happens through one of several ways: death, gaining legal status, leaving the country voluntarily, and deportation. The average number of entrants each year during this time was 706,000, and the average number of departures was 356,000. Formal removals, which include deportations, exclusions, and removals, had steadily risen during the decade. In 1990, only 30,039 people were removed; in 1999, there were nearly 181,000 formal removals.

Taking the Risk to Immigrate

Undocumented immigrants enter the United States knowing they probably won't be able to fully take part in American society. They can't vote, and they can't legally get a job or receive a number of other entitlements that citizens and legal immigrants take for granted. Still, so many undocumented immigrants arrive and stay each year. Even more are caught trying to enter the country. With so much stacked against them, why do they take the risk?

For many foreign nationals, the idea of living in the United States seems better than living in their own country, and in many cases, they are right. Some people immigrate from countries torn apart by war, ruled by repressive regimes, or divided by ethnic strife. Citizens in these countries may have a genuine fear for their life and safety. Under certain circumstances, these people are deemed asylum seekers. If they make it to the United States— even illegally—they can apply for and be granted asylum.

Others immigrate because their nations' economies may offer few opportunities, particularly to those who are driven to succeed. A common characteristic of most immigrants is risk-taking, and often poverty drives them to take the greatest risks. Even if they do not have official working papers, there may be more job opportunities in the United States than in their native land. Statistical levels of poverty in the United States can sometimes paint an inexact picture, since poor immigrants to the country are often still better off than those who remain in developing countries.

Many immigrants take the risk to enter the United States for the freedoms the country offers. Americans enjoy freedom of speech, freedom of movement, and freedom of religion. These are the purest gifts the nation has to offer, and many of those who lacked them in their home country appreciate their value.

Finally, immigrants are attracted by the broad appeal of American culture, which continually projects an image of freedom and wealth. Foreign television channels show American sitcoms, and there are billboards for Coca-Cola and other products in almost every nation of the world. This constant exposure stirs a hunger for a more direct contact with American culture.

Where They Come From and How They Enter

Most undocumented immigrants are from Latin America. According to the INS's 2003 report, in 2000 over 4.8 million

Russians eat at a McDonald's restaurant in the capital city of Moscow. In some major international cities, investments made by American and other Western corporations have revitalized economic districts. An indirect result of this growth among immigrants has been an awareness of American culture and the opportunities that living in the United States may offer.

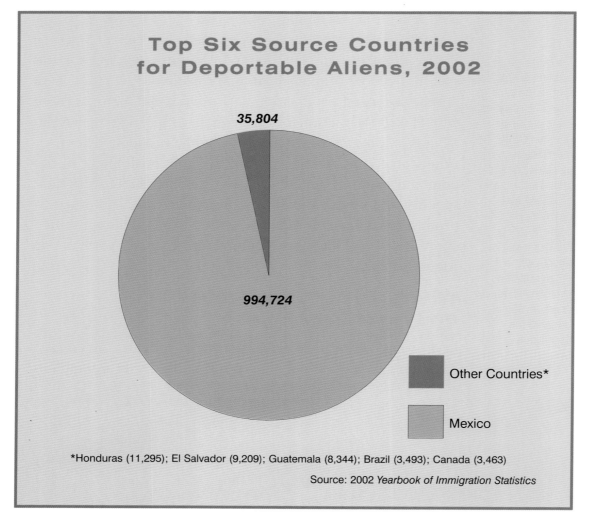

Top Six Source Countries for Deportable Aliens, 2002

35,804

994,724

Other Countries*

Mexico

*Honduras (11,295); El Salvador (9,209); Guatemala (8,344); Brazil (3,493); Canada (3,463)

Source: 2002 *Yearbook of Immigration Statistics*

out of an estimated 7 million undocumented immigrants were Mexican nationals. Mexico's Central American neighbors are also source countries of great numbers of immigrants, although nowhere near the totals of Mexicans. Approximately 189,000 Salvadoran undocumented immigrants lived in the United States in 2000. This number had dropped from the nearly 300,000 in 1990. Other large Central and South American undocumented immigrant populations hail from Guatemala, with 144,000 people recorded in 2000; Colombia, 141,000; and Honduras, 138,000. The Chinese undocumented group totaled 115,000 people. Other top countries in this category are Ecuador, the Dominican Republic, the Philippines, Brazil, Haiti, India, Peru, Korea, and Canada.

Most undocumented aliens arrive into the country by bypassing inspection one way or another. In 2002, of the more than 1,062,000 deportable aliens located by the Department of Homeland Security, more than 1,031,000 people had entered without inspection, according to the 2002 *Yearbook of Immigration Statistics*.

Overseas smuggling is one way to enter the United States without inspection, particularly for undocumented immigrants

Asian migrants are discovered by U.S. Coast Guardsmen in the cargo hold of a ship in the Northern Hawaiian Islands, 1999. Stowing away in the cramped space of a ship is a typical—though often dangerous—method of illegal migration.

from China and other Asian countries. Smugglers, often referred to as "snakeheads," have continually brought Chinese nationals across the Pacific on ships. Snakeheads charge anywhere from $15,000 to $35,000 per passenger, high fees indicating the desperation that immigrants feel.

Chinese immigrants are not the only ones that consider the option of smuggling. Snakeheads squeeze migrants from India and Pakistan into cargo holds of ships. Other ships come from the Caribbean with secret cargos of Haitians or Dominicans. Salvadorans and Nicaraguans are brought from South America.

To avoid detection, smugglers may build false walls around the inside of their hulls. The cargo bay that is visible may hold a legal import, such as sugar or fruit. Immigrants have completed an entire trip hidden in the cramped space between the walls and the hull.

Needless to say, smuggling is extremely dangerous, and not nearly as common a form of entry as arriving via plane or on foot across the Mexican or Canadian border. Many passengers on ships have to endure the entire journey standing up. Usually, the space is so small they can't turn around or lift their arms. If anything happens to the ship, there are few ways for the passengers to reach safety. They could drown encased in the secret hull.

The passengers of the *Golden Venture* faced a situation like this one in a tragic water accident in 1993. The Chinese freighter, a ship involved in a snakehead operation smuggling Chinese nationals into the United States, ran aground on Rockaway Beach in Queens, New York. The journey from China took 112 days, far longer than expected. Nearly 300 hungry and exhausted passengers were forced to swim 200 yards to shore; 10 of them didn't make it, either drowning or dying of hypothermia. The survivors were picked up and detained by the INS. Many were granted asylum, but some returned to China or settled in other countries. According to the Associated Press, 38 *Golden Venture* passengers have been denied asylum but are still in the country. They were deportable, although they had received work permits from the

A group of Mexicans approaches the U.S. border at Agua Prieta, Mexico. Migrants attempting to illegally enter the country may try to cross the border undetected or pass through an official port of entry using fake documents that are stolen or purchased.

government and were unlikely to be a high priority for deportation.

Evading the Law

About 40 percent of undocumented immigrants enter the country legally and then stay past the time limit that was decided on at a port of entry. For example, a person arriving on a tourist visa is usually permitted to stay six months. Someone who enters from one of the more than 25 countries participating in the Visa Waiver Program can enter without a visa and stay for 90 days. A foreign student is not given a specific period of time but must continue to pursue a full course of study or he or she will be considered "out of status."

Some entrants try to use false documents to get past immigration inspectors. These can be either custom-made forgeries with false information or genuine passports of someone other than the holder. Technological changes have made forgery more difficult, but forgers are always searching for new strategies.

While some fake documents are homemade, the most effective ones are official papers that have received some slight changes. U.S. passports can be stolen or purchased from Americans for $1,000 or more. Immigration inspectors have expert training in detecting fraudulent documents; however, the enormous volume of travelers every day means that even with a high detection rate of false documents many people will still enter the country who should not.

Some migrants who aim to use false IDs first look through the obituaries of U.S. newspapers. After finding deceased people who match their own age and gender, the migrants base false identification information on them. Then they will pose as a family member in order to obtain extra birth certificates. When a migrant presents a false ID with a genuine birth certificate to an inspector, the fake ID will look all the more genuine.

Undocumented immigrants may find relief in having successfully crossed the border, but in many respects, they have

Biometric BCCs

For years, immigration authorities have permitted aliens to cross the Mexican border for short visits to shop or visit relatives, as long as they present a border control card. A clause of the 1996 Illegal Immigration Reform and Immigrant Responsibility Act called for Mexican visitors to carry an updated, machine-readable ID card. These cards are known as biometric Border Control Cards, or BCCs for short. They are laminated and are the size of a credit card. On the front of the card is a photograph, valid for 10 years; on the back is a magnetic strip with additional information. To get a BCC, an applicant has to go to a consulate to be photographed and fingerprinted. Then the application is sent to the INS, which issues the card.

Biometric BCCs were first issued in 1998, as the old cards were being phased out. In October 2002, the new cards became the only acceptable version. More than 5 million biometric BCCs have been issued as of this writing.

Undocumented immigrants typically find jobs, like this maintenance worker's, that may not require great scrutiny of their credentials. Other typical fields of employment for undocumented immigrants are farm labor, landscaping, garment making, and domestic service.

only reached the hard stage. Once across the border, life becomes a matter of remaining undetected, and if they want to find work or buy a home, they have to conceal their true identities.

It is illegal for an employer to "knowingly" hire an individual who is not authorized to work in the country. An employer is required to check certain documents provided by the worker and ask him or her questions to fill out what is known as an I-9 form. However, employers are not expert at catching fraudulent documents, which is encouraging for many undocumented immigrants.

To avoid detection in the workplace, undocumented immigrants often find work where people don't ask too many questions. In major U.S. cities there are street corner labor markets where undocumented immigrants may huddle on a corner until a truck pulls over looking for workers for the day. Although this kind of "shadow economy" may provide temporary employment, no one is guaranteed a job from one day to the next.

Most undocumented immigrants fill jobs that people with other options often wouldn't take for long periods of time. Typical jobs include harvesting crops, landscaping, garment making, kitchen work, lower-level construction, and domestic service, such as working as a maid.

There have been cases of employers mistreating immigrants that go beyond the bounds of "poor working conditions." In 1979 a man was arrested for keeping two undocumented immigrants workers chained on his chicken farm. There have been many cases in which women were brought to the United States for maid work who were then forced into prostitution. And in 2001, 36 people were convicted of trafficking in humans as virtual slaves. Each defendant had brought people into the United States on false pretenses and sold or kept them for forced labor. Migrants who are victims of this kind of exploitation cannot be deported while their perpetrators are on trial, and if they are victims of human trafficking, they may be allowed to stay in the United States.

Where Undocumented Immigrants Settle

The INS study of the unauthorized immigrant population, released in January 2003, reported that of the 7 million undocumented aliens living in the United States in 2000, California was estimated to hold 2.2 million, or nearly one-third of the group's population. Texas had the second-highest total, with 1.04 million, followed by New York (489,000), Illinois (432,000), and Florida (337,000).

While California took in more undocumented immigrants between 1990 and 2000, the percentage of the undocumented population settling in California had decreased from 42 percent to 32 percent during those years. This statistic suggests that undocumented immigrants had spread out around the country, with Illinois and Texas receiving a greater percentage of the group. Even relatively small populations of undocumented immigrants, such as those in Colorado, New Jersey, and North Carolina, received a proportional boost. Colorado's population quadrupled in size, and North Carolina's grew to almost eight times its size, from an estimated 26,000 undocumented aliens to 206,000.

4 WHO GETS DEPORTED?

The Immigration and Nationality Act outlines 20 categories of deportable aliens. Counting the subcategories within each of these categories, there are nearly 700 grounds for deportation. Some distinctions between grounds are fine points of law, while others are very broad.

Types of Deportation

The grounds for deportation can be divided into three basic types: acts committed before, during, and after entry into the United States. Most deportations occur during entry.

After aliens are apprehended and go through an interview, officials decide whether to keep them in custody or order them to return to the country they most recently left. Most who receive the latter ruling leave the country voluntarily. Those who are kept in custody are given a removal hearing.

One deportable action that can take place before entry is fraud, of which a common type is marriage fraud. Foreign nationals sometimes fake marriages in order to be granted an entry visa. Agents have the authority to investigate a suspect marriage. If they can prove the marriage is false, the alien may face deportation and the U.S. citizen may face charges of fraud. In 2002, 41,057 people were deported or excluded for fraud, misrepresentation, or entering without proper documents.

Former members of Germany's Nazi Party fit into another

◀ Members of a Japanese-American family await evacuation from their Hayward, California, home to an internment camp in this May 1942 photograph. In a controversial decision made during World War II, the U.S. government interred and deported Japanese Americans in the interest of national security.

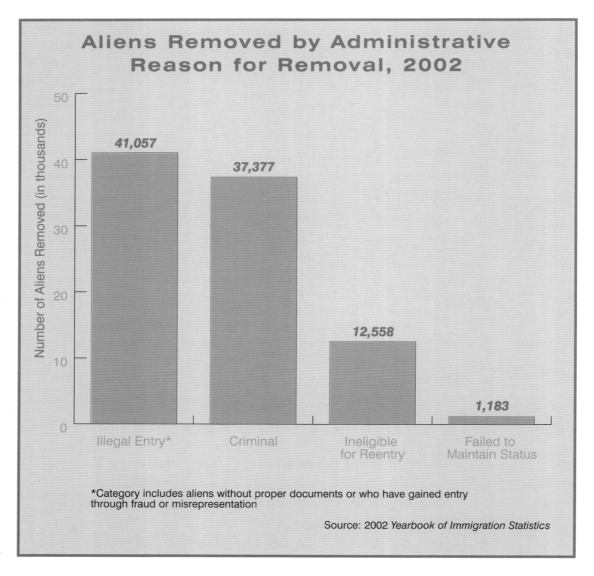

Aliens Removed by Administrative Reason for Removal, 2002

Number of Aliens Removed (in thousands)

Illegal Entry*	Criminal	Ineligible for Reentry	Failed to Maintain Status
41,057	37,377	12,558	1,183

*Category includes aliens without proper documents or who have gained entry through fraud or misrepresentation

Source: 2002 *Yearbook of Immigration Statistics*

class of deportable alien. A 1978 amendment to the Immigration and Nationality Act states that anyone who as part of the Nazi Party "ordered, incited, assisted, or otherwise participated in the persecution of any person because of race, religion, national origin, or opinion" can face deportation.

A number of former Nazis came to the United States before their crimes were deemed deportable offenses, but that was of no consequence. Grounds for deportation are retroactive, which means that any committed act that later becomes grounds for deportation can be used to deport an alien, even if he or she entered before the change was instituted. If a ground for deportation does not include a timeframe, the act or condition can be used against a person at any point in his or her life. For this reason, Nazis can be deported 50 years after they committed war crimes.

One catchall phase that applies to aliens who commit deportable actions before entering is "excludable at the time of entry." There are 33 different classes of aliens whose condition or behavior, if known, can keep them from entering the United States. Sometimes people manage to gain admittance even when exclusion laws should have kept them out. In those cases, it is still legal for that person to be deported at a later date.

This identity card of former Nazi death camp guard John Demjanjuks, who immigrated to the United States in 1952, served as evidence in the decision to revoke his citizenship in February 2002. Demjanjuks' family appealed the decision, postponing the motion to deport the elderly man back to his native Ukraine.

John Lennon

A few years after his band the Beatles broke up, John Lennon moved from England to New York City. He came to the country on a visitor's visa in August 1968, and after renewing his visa several times, he planned to become a lawful permanent resident.

Those plans were stalled when the FBI placed him under surveillance in December 1971. The world-famous rock singer had appeared at a benefit concert that month for John Sinclair, a political activist who had been sentenced to a lengthy jail period of 10 years for marijuana possession. The well-attended concert served as an example of the political influence Lennon had on young people, and in particular, how he could affect public opinion on U.S. involvement in the Vietnam War. After the benefit show Lennon began expressing interest in holding voter-registration stands at rock concerts.

The rock star's influence alarmed some government leaders. They knew that young voters could potentially change the balance of power in Washington, and could help vote President Richard Nixon out of office. To address this threat, the FBI began investigating Lennon and his activist friends. There is no proof of President Nixon's involvement in the investigations; however, it has been revealed that J. Edgar Hoover, the director of the FBI, wrote one of Nixon's top advisors about the Lennon project.

Soon after the investigation began, the FBI turned up Lennon's criminal record. In an English court Lennon had pled guilty to possessing marijuana. Because he had been convicted of a drug charge, technically he could have been kept from entering the country in the first place. As an excludable alien, Lennon was also deportable, and so the INS gave him 60 days to leave the country.

Some deportable grounds apply to voluntary behaviors. For example, if the alien is a drug addict, a polygamist, a prostitute, or has committed crimes "of moral turpitude" (depravity), he or she can be excluded. Other excludable individuals have conditions they cannot control. The insane, the mentally retarded, and people with certain highly contagious diseases can be prohibited from entering the United States.

Lennon could afford much better lawyers than the typical immigrant, and they managed to consistently get his stay extended. But in the meantime, they gave simple advice to Lennon: don't do anything more to attract the FBI's attention.

Lennon abandoned his idea of voter-registration concerts. In 1974, Richard Nixon resigned after the Watergate scandal was uncovered. Under his successor, Gerald Ford, the INS finally stopped pursing Lennon's deportation. After some legal wrangling, Lennon was awarded lawful permanent resident status in 1976.

John Lennon flashes the peace sign before entering a New York INS office to appeal his deportation, May 1972.

Subversives and Other Deportable Aliens

Most deportation grounds deal with an alien's conduct within the United States, which makes logical sense for a majority of people. For much of its history the United States has been a place to make a new start for so many immigrants; by that logic, an individual's past is less important than what he or she

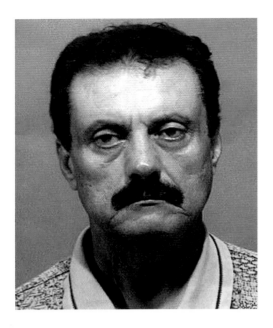

Millionaire Palestinian American Jesse Maali was charged with immigration violations and other crimes in November 2002. Because Maali was suspected of having financial links with terrorist organizations, he faced deportation as a potential subversive.

does within the new country's borders. However, subversives are one group of people who can be prosecuted for conduct within the United States. Individuals who oppose all organized government, also known as anarchists, are considered subversives, as are communists and their supporters. When someone threatens national security or advocates the violent overthrow of the U.S. government—which includes writing or publishing subversive materials—he or she is committing a subversive act. Potential terrorists, assassins, spies, and saboteurs are all classified as subversives. The law gives the attorney general discretion in identifying members of this class.

Aliens who receive a prison sentence for at least a year in the United States, or who are convicted of more than one crime, also may face deportation. A very broad ground for deportation is "crimes of moral turpitude." Aliens do not have to serve time for these particular crimes in order for them to be deportable offenses, which means the deportation hearing can begin immediately after they are handed their prison sentence.

In 2002, 37,377 people were deported for criminal activity. Most deportable crimes threaten the health and safety of U.S. citizens. Prostitution and associated crimes are deportable offenses, as are drug and weapons convictions. An alien can be deported for possessing an illegal weapon or for having, smuggling, or selling drugs.

Finally, there are immigration law violations that can occur before and after an alien has entered the country. Deportable offenses of the latter kind include violating visa conditions, falsifying immigration documents, helping other aliens enter the country, and failing to report to immigration authorities for a requested meeting. Even failure to report a change of address within 30 days of a request is a deportable offense. In the years following the September 2001 attacks, the U.S. government has used many of these kinds of technical violations to deport individuals suspected to be national security threats.

5 AT THE BORDER

Over a million people try to enter the country without authorization each year. It is the duty of the Border Patrol, part of the Bureau of Customs and Border Protection (BCBP) within the Department of Homeland Security, to patrol U.S. borders and apprehend or deter illegal entry. The Border Patrol is also responsible to stop drug smuggling over the border.

Given the length of the U.S. northern and southern borders, enforcement is a challenging undertaking. The Border Patrol has divided the border and coastline areas into sectors. The nine sectors in the Southwest—nearly 2,000 miles of the Mexican line—are the busiest.

Between the lawful ports of entry in the Southwest are many miles of border. Agents patrol the line in jeeps, trucks, and other all-terrain vehicles. Others keep a watch over popular crossing areas on foot. Some agents are visible, patrolling the Rio Grande in motorboats, while others are camouflaged, staking out assigned territory from behind desert shrubs.

The 2002 *Yearbook of Immigration Statistics* reported that during that year, the Border Patrol apprehended over 955,000 illegal entrants, an average of over 79,500 per month. All but 25,500 were apprehended in the Southwest region. Despite the many captures made by the Border Patrol, the government reports that many illegal entrants make it through and stay

◀ A U.S. Border Patrol agent ushers two undocumented immigrants into custody in Douglas, Arizona. Border agents, particularly those employed in the Southwest states of Texas, Arizona, New Mexico, and California, routinely deal with illegal crossing attempts.

each year. Agents can't be everywhere at once, so they greatly rely on technology. Video cameras transmit images of the border to patrol outposts. Helicopters monitor wide stretches of land, directing ground crews to trouble areas. Electronic sensors detect motion or vibrations in the ground.

Border Patrol Agents are also trained to follow trails left by entrants. They keep a clear eye for footprints, litter, and other signs of human activity. To make footprints far more visible and difficult to cover up, agents drag mats behind their jeeps, smoothing out the ground.

Policing Operations

In the 1990s, the Border Patrol began using new tactics to halt illegal border crossings. The new approaches began in specific sectors in the Southwest that were later expanded to include more areas. One program, Operation Hold The Line, was initiated in the El Paso, Texas, sector. Instead of chasing down migrants who cross the border, the operation aimed to deter them from crossing at all. Agents were stationed in plain sight, each one patrolling a half-mile segment of border. Since the El Paso border has flat terrain, each agent could see and be seen from a great distance. With an agent usually in sight, fewer people risked crossing. In the operation's first three years, the number of apprehensions dropped by half. The operation was clearly working in the area it was implemented, yet it still did not decrease overall unauthorized entry into the United States.

Following the advent of Operation Hold the Line, INS launched Operation Rio Grande, which essentially expanded Hold The Line into two more sectors. The INS hired new agents to man the border. It also began using new technology, including night-vision goggles, infrared scopes, and an automated fingerprint system called IDENT. In addition, better roads were constructed along the border, which gave the agents better access to situations arising in remote locations.

In San Diego, a different program called Operation Gatekeeper took shape that addressed the unique demands of

A well-lit fence divides the border between Tijuana, Mexico, and San Ysidro, California. The newly constructed fence was one of the technical improvements that emerged from Operation Gatekeeper, first implemented in 1994.

the terrain around the city. Unlike the El Paso border, the San Diego landscape is crowded and visibility is limited. Also, the El Paso sector abuts the Rio Grande, while San Diego has no such natural border. Only a fence divides the U.S. and Mexico sides there. Beyond that fence are ravines and heavy undergrowth in which there are hundreds of places to hide.

Operation Gatekeeper was initiated in the fall of 1994. Initially, the operation was tested on a five-mile stretch of border called Imperial Beach. Its success convinced officials to expand it throughout the 66 miles of the sector stretching eastward from San Diego to El Centro.

The first improvements were made to the hardware along the border. Multiple fences were erected. Where before undocumented immigrants had to climb one 16-foot fence, now they had to climb three. And they would have to do it quickly, since the bright lights on the fences would keep them exposed until they completely climbed over the last fence. For those immigrants not in plain view, border guards used infrared scopes, and relied on high-tech sensors that could detect movement and group size.

New hardware on the border also obstructed attempts to tunnel under the fence. Deep steel plates were installed to stop tunnels at midpoint. In addition to the technological advances, the number of border personnel was beefed up. By 1996, the San Diego–El Centro area had 1,300 agents.

These programs had their critics, who argued that by making the trek over the border more difficult, enforcement had made smuggling enterprises all the more profitable. Of even greater concern is the increase in migrant deaths, believed to have been indirectly caused by the channeling of illegal entrants into more dangerous areas. In 2000, the Border Patrol reported an alarming total of 383 border-crossing deaths in that year alone. Annual death totals have stayed high since that time.

Many people still support the deterrence of illegal border crossings, having found that easy-to-cross areas consistently

A U.S. Border Patrol agent patrols a remote border section west of Tucson, Arizona. In 1995 Operation Safeguard was launched. Similar to the programs in Texas and California, Operation Safeguard sought to move potential crossers away from urban areas along the Arizona border to more remote locations where they are easier to locate.

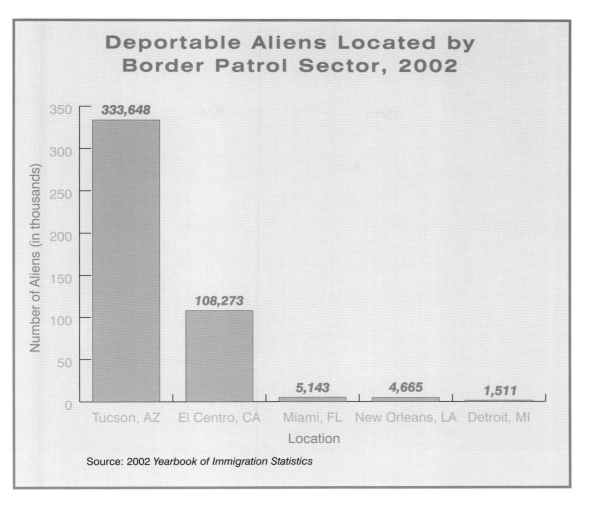

Deportable Aliens Located by Border Patrol Sector, 2002

Number of Aliens (in thousands)

Tucson, AZ	333,648
El Centro, CA	108,273
Miami, FL	5,143
New Orleans, LA	4,665
Detroit, MI	1,511

Location

Source: 2002 *Yearbook of Immigration Statistics*

attract more entrants. But tracking the effectiveness of these programs remains difficult, for the primary reason that migrant movements change over time. What remains unclear is how much these efforts truly lower the number of unlawful entries, or if they simply redirect the same numbers to other places.

Critics of tough immigration laws suggest that the issue of illegal migration is primarily an economical one of supply and demand. U.S. employers offer more jobs, and eager workers find better opportunities than those found in their home country. These critics argue that efforts to create additional avenues for workers to enter legally, which have been discussed by President George W. Bush and Mexican president Vicente Fox,

may do more to prevent illegal crossings than any law enforcement strategy could.

Crossing the Mexican Border

Walking over the border into the United States is the most common way to illegally enter the country. Many more people enter the country illegally through Mexico than through Canada. Over 95 percent of border-crossing arrests in the past 10 years have been in the Southwest. Well over 90 percent of the people apprehended by the U.S. Border Patrol on the Southwest border are Mexicans; the remaining 10 percent are comprised of people from all over the world.

People attempting to illegally cross the border need to plan ahead. Their best chance at success is to sneak in under the

Mexican president Vicente Fox and President George W. Bush speak to reporters outside the White House in Washington, D.C. In September 2001 the two leaders discussed how to create more job opportunities for Mexican workers as a way to decrease illegal migration.

cover of night. Most loiter around unguarded areas of the border until nightfall. Like those entering by sea, people entering by foot often hire smugglers to get them across. These smugglers are called "coyotes" in border slang. (The undocumented immigrants they smuggle are often called *pollos*, the Spanish word for "chickens.")

The work of the average smuggler can entail all kinds of tasks. It can be as simple as carrying a woman across the strong currents of the Rio Grande, or something more involved, like taking a group of *pollos* across the border, setting them up at a safe house, and finding them jobs. Coyotes charge around $500 for a simple drive across the border. Other services cost more. In her book *Illegal Immigration*, author Kathleen Lee reveals that coyotes can get up to $5,000 for a full-service operation, complete with a safe house, English lessons, and a job. Some coyotes even take a percentage of the immigrants' pay once they have arrived and found employment.

In recent years, the U.S. Border Patrol has recorded the cause of death for migrants illegally crossing the U.S.–Mexico border. Between 2000 and 2002, heat exposure was the leading cause of death.

Migrant Deaths by Type, 1999–2002

Type of Death	1999	2000	2001	2002
Exposure-Heat	59	144	123	137
Exposure-Cold	17	17	4	7
Train	17	5	3	2
Car Accident	22	48	27	28
Confined Space	1	0	0	2
Drowning	76	95	74	58
Unknown	41	47	97	77
Other	17	27	8	9
Total	**250**	**383**	**336**	**320**

Source: U.S. Border Patrol

Coyotes will often work in teams, in which case members will get paid individually each time one of them performs a task for the migrants. One smuggler may bring the immigrants across the river; the next may pack them into a truck and bring them further into the country. Smugglers often use big vans or trucks with no windows. A number of smugglers have been blamed for abandoning migrants in the desert or in other unsafe areas, thereby endangering many lives.

As with smuggling on the seas, smuggling across the border is dangerous. Many migrants die in car accidents. A typical rear-ender that usually results in few or no injuries can prove to be fatal when someone is hiding in the trunk of the car. Coyote vans can be packed just as tightly as smuggling ships. With no ventilation, vehicles can heat up like ovens. Migrants have died

A Mexican man is discovered sewn in the back seat of a van in an attempt to evade border patrol officials. Undocumented immigrants who are smuggled across the U.S.–Mexico border in vans and trucks risk suffocation and dangerously high temperatures.

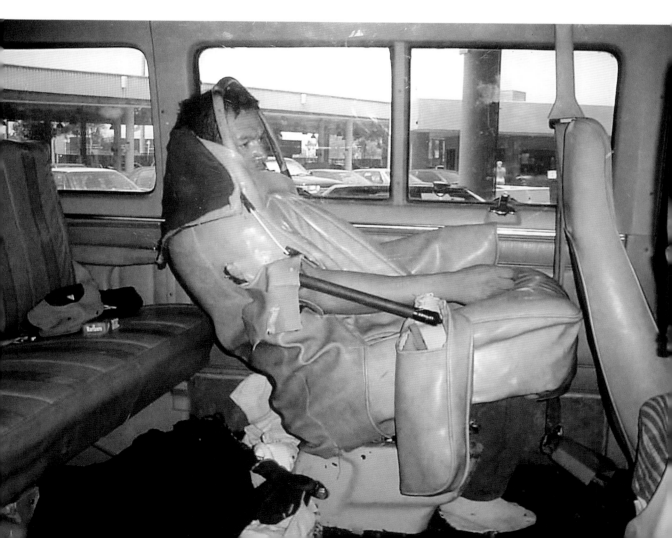

of heat exposure and suffocation. Yet even when the situation is desperate, sometimes they don't call out for help. They fear that if they make any noise, they will be caught and sent home.

Bandits are yet another danger for migrants. Central Americans waiting in Mexico to cross into the United States have complained of being set upon by bandits, some of whom were reported to be corrupt Mexican police officers. People have been robbed, beaten, or worse by the criminals. Sometimes bandits will collaborate with smugglers, who will lead the migrants straight to the robbers.

6 OTHER ENFORCEMENT METHODS

In recent decades, the U.S. government has required American employers to play a part in immigration enforcement. The 1986 Immigration Reform and Control Act (IRCA) made it the responsibility of employers to check for proof of work eligibility before hiring someone. If they do not perform this check, they may face sanctions.

Today, only certain documents can prove eligibility for employment in the United States. These include the U.S. passport and documents issued by immigration authorities, such as the alien resident card. Employers must ask for these documents when they hire people; however, they are not held responsible for missing any forgeries or falsifications on the information they are given, as long as they review the documents in good faith.

When the Immigration Reform and Control Act was passed, some employers protested. They claimed that checking for undocumented immigrants was not their responsibility but the responsibility of the federal government. Civil rights groups also balked, arguing that in an attempt to faithfully follow the law, some employers may avoid hiring Latinos on the chance that they are undocumented and will slip through the interview with false papers.

◀A woman shakes hands after a job interview. All job applicants in the United States must present identification to prove their legal status. Since the passing of the Immigrant Reform and Control Act (IRCA) in 1986, employers have been held responsible for checking the official documents of job candidates.

Marriage Fraud and Criminal Tracking

Immigration officials are continually pressed to enforce measures against marriage fraud. Because spouses and fiancés/fiancées of U.S. citizens are eligible for visas that let them live and work in the United States, it is common for two people to attempt marriage fraud so one of them can illegally enter the country.

There has been a sharp rise in fiancé/fiancée admissions in recent years. In the early and mid-1980s, there were only a few hundred of these kinds of visas issued each year. In 2000, the number was 20,000, and it jumped to over 23,000 the following year. An undetermined portion of these marriages is fraudulent. Some false marriages are arranged by smugglers, while others are set up independently.

The Bureau of Immigration and Customs Enforcement (BICE) is authorized to investigate transnational marriages for possible fraud. Sometimes BICE officers have discovered that the couple has been living apart, and that they barely see each other, if at all. Most couples committing fraud are savvy enough to use a joint address even if they don't live together, since separate mailing addresses are a sure tip-off for investigators.

A common approach to determining whether or not a marriage is legitimate is to bring the man and the woman in for questioning. BICE officials conduct the interviews of the spouses separately. The questions range from mundane, everyday matters to personal details about their relationship. Most married people know a lot of details about their spouses. If the interviewees are evasive, or off base with their answers, their marriage may be deemed fraudulent.

Proving that a marriage is fraudulent with convincing evidence is no easy task, however. There are typically many gray-area questions: How many wrong answers indicate that the partners don't love each other? What separates a phony marriage from a genuine, failed union? This matter is often left for the courts to decide. In 2001, there were over 1,800 cases where marriage fraud was found to have taken place in the United States.

Some undocumented immigrants are caught and detained before immigration officers have come into contact with them. Under cooperative programs with local and state prison officials, BICE personnel are notified when undocumented immigrants and permanent residents who are deportable have completed their criminal sentences. However, given the size of the United States and the limited resources of both the localities and federal investigative authorities, not all individuals are successfully taken into immigration enforcement custody after they complete their sentences. Such lapses have received public criticism.

7 DEPORTATION PROCEEDINGS

The arrest of a deportable alien is the first major step of a deportation proceeding. In many ways, the alien's arrest is similar to the arrest of a criminal. An officer must inform aliens why they are being arrested, that their statements may be used against them, and that they have the right to an attorney. At a later point, they must be told if they will be kept in custody or released on bond.

Most aliens served with warrants are not jailed and instead are released on bond of $500 or more, or on good faith that they will appear in court. Some aliens are released on conditional parole as well, which means that if their situation changes, the parole or bond can be canceled at any time.

Aliens who are jailed are placed in one of the immigration holding facilities located in five states and in Puerto Rico. When these facilities are filled up, federal prisons take in the detainees. Aliens are usually held because they have been determined to be at risk of running from the law if they are released. Agents consider many factors when determining flight risk, such as aliens' arrest records in the United States and the countries from which they have emigrated. There are other conditions that make aliens less likely to flee, such as steady employment or responsibilities to family members living in the United States.

There is much debate over the practice of holding aliens in

◄ These detainees at a holding center in Brownsville, Texas, have illegally entered the United States through Mexico and are waiting to be processed. Similar detention centers are located in Puerto Rico and the states of New York, California, Arizona, and Florida.

custody. Supporters of detention argue that it is the surest way of keeping a careful watch over someone who is facing a possible deportation sentence. But some detractors argue that the government uses an excessive amount of its resources to hold aliens for extended periods.

One group of aliens that greatly concern immigration enforcement officials are absconders, individuals who fail to report after the authorities have issued a final order of deportation. In 2002, there were an estimated 300,000 or more individuals who did not comply with deportation orders. The INS Commissioner at the time, Jim Ziglar, responded to the situation by announcing the Alien Absconder Initiative, which aimed to track down these individuals. While the measure has been partially successful and has received some support, the task has been daunting given the limited investigative resources and the difficulty of finding many absconders.

Aliens alleged to be involved in subversive or terrorist activities are usually held without bond. A judge's decision to permit bond can be challenged all the way up to the attorney general, who in immigration proceedings retains the ultimate authority over these decisions. In some cases, the Department of Homeland Security may deem suspected terrorists to be threats to national security, and will make decisions based on information that is kept secret from the public.

Beginning the Procedure

The deportation procedure begins when an arrest warrant is issued. The warrant automatically triggers another form, called an Order to Show Cause, which is the government's formal request to the alien to prove why he or she should remain in the country. Any alien who cannot fulfill this request will face a removal hearing.

The Order to Show Cause cannot be issued without evidence of deportability. It can be served to an alien either in person or through the mail. The order itself must contain specific information, included a statement of the charges against the alien, as well as the specific facts of his or her violation. A full removal hearing can take months to schedule. Because many aliens speak poor English, or none at all, it is often difficult to mount a good defense by themselves. They can use the time before the hearing to find a lawyer and prepare their case.

Rights of the Alien

Under the law, aliens are guaranteed certain rights in the procedures before and during the deportation hearing. Along with the right to know the nature of the charges and the time and place of the hearing, they also have a right to be present for the hearing. However, if they fail to make an appearance the court can still proceed and reach a decision in their absence.

As in criminal trials, aliens who undergo deportation hearings have the right to present evidence in their favor, and to examine evidence presented against them (except in rare cases involving classified evidence.) They can present oral or written testimony, and their counsel can cross-examine government witnesses. They can even use a subpoena, a judge's order to an unwilling witness to testify.

There is a right that an alien, unlike the criminal defendant, only has under certain circumstances in a removal hearing, which is the right to refuse to testify against oneself. This is commonly known as "pleading the Fifth Amendment" or "pleading the Fifth." An immigration judge can demand that aliens answer questions directed toward them. The only circumstance under which an alien may plead the Fifth is if his or her alleged actions are criminal in addition to being violations of immigration law.

Removal hearings are open to the public, unless an immigration judge decides otherwise. In the months after the September 2001 terrorist attacks, the Department of Justice under Attorney General John Ashcroft incited controversy by closing immigration hearings to the public, stating it was necessary for national security. Critics have charged that while there may have been a need for such secrecy in the early days after

September 11, the continuation of the policy was aimed more at hiding flaws in processing people who, it turned out, only in rare cases had any terrorist connections.

In the situation that the alien doesn't speak English, a court interpreter is appointed to the hearing. The interpreter's performance is crucial to the fairness of the trial. Yet even with an interpreter, it can be difficult for the alien to understand the legal jargon that is used throughout the hearing. If an alien believes that an interpreter has been incompetent, he or she can appeal a ruling, but only after presenting convincing evidence.

Aliens are entitled to legal representation, also called counsel. If they do not have counsel on the day of the hearing, the immigration judge may postpone the hearing so that he or she has time to find one. Unlike in criminal cases, the government will not provide or pay for an attorney, but there are various advocacy organizations that provide free legal services for immigrants proven to be in need. Still, many undocumented immigrants do not retain attorneys, and their success rate is significantly lower than that of aliens who are represented.

The alien's counsel does not have to be a certified lawyer, although many are. Law school graduates—and in some cases, even law students who have not yet passed the bar exam—may act as counsel. The Board of Immigration Appeals (BIA) has also approved representatives of certain organizations to act as counsel. Finally, an alien may receive counsel from an attorney living in a foreign country, or a representative of his or her home government.

The Deportation Hearing

The alien's counsel faces off with an attorney from the Bureau of Immigration and Customs Enforcement. The job of these attorneys is similar to that of a prosecutor in a criminal trial. They must convince the judge that the facts of the case call for deportation, and like prosecutors, they can present evidence, call on witnesses, and cross-examine other witnesses to prove their case. Immigration judges are selected by the attorney general,

In June 2002 U.S. Attorney General John Ashcroft (right) ordered that in the interest of national security, the immigration hearings of terrorism suspects would be closed to the public. The decision incited controversy among critics who accused the Department of Justice of trying to hide flaws in the proceedings.

and they are usually former trial attorneys for the government. They have the authority to order depositions, issue subpoenas, and rule on the admissibility of evidence.

The official hearing begins with the reading the charges against the alien, and one more reminder of his or her rights. As author David Weissbrodt describes in his book *Immigration Law and Procedure in a Nutshell*, the alien must then pick a country to be sent to, should he or she be deported. (Making this choice is not an admission of deportability.) The immigration judge then chooses an alternate country. If a deported alien's first choice does not accept him or her, the alternate country will receive the alien. This selection can be a controversial matter in itself, since the country that is chosen may be experiencing civil war or has an oppressive government that threatens the alien's safety.

A Young Cuban's Removal

In November 1999, a six-year-old boy named Elián González was rescued at sea off the coast of Florida. His mother had brought him in an attempt to escape Cuba and request asylum in the United States.

The ship had capsized and Elián was the only survivor. A Florida fisherman had found the boy, who had been floating in an inner tube for two days. Soon Elián was paroled into the country and put into the custody of his great-uncle, Lazaro González, in Miami. Lazaro then filed an asylum application on Elián's behalf.

Elián's father, Juan Miguel González-Quintana, learned what had happened and asked that his son be returned to Cuba, a request that ignited a heated debate over asylum. Could Lazaro truly speak for Elián if the boy's father wanted something else? It was a legitimate question. But then again, could it be certain that Juan Miguel, a citizen living under an oppressive regime, was speaking freely in his request?

Elián's father and the relatives in Miami became locked in a fierce legal struggle that moved from court to court. First, the INS denied Elián's asylum claims and ordered his return to Cuba. The relatives in Miami responded by suing, which delayed Elián's return, keeping him in their home. In April 2000, Elián's father flew to the United States to meet his son.

Then, following an order given by Attorney General Janet Reno, Justice Department agents stormed the Miami home in the early hours of April 23. They took Elián away from his relatives at gunpoint and returned him to his father, with whom he remained until the case was decided. In June, the legal dust finally settled when the U.S. Supreme Court refused to overturn a circuit court ruling against the relatives, after which Elián returned to Cuba with his father.

After making this decision about a destination, the alien is then allowed to apply for discretionary relief, which is a formal request to a judge to set aside the deportation procedure because of special circumstances. In many cases, the alien offers to leave the country voluntarily to avoid the stigma of deportation, which threatens the success of a future attempt to legally enter the United States. Then, the government must prove that the alien is indeed an alien and not a U.S. citizen or national, who under law cannot be deported. If the trial attorney fails to prove this status, the case must be thrown out.

After going through these preliminary procedures, it is time for the alien to present evidence that establishes his or her right to remain in the country. The trial attorney will attempt to counter the alien's evidence. If he or she cannot, the judge must rule in favor of the alien. The judge can order the deportation, end the deportation proceedings (allowing the alien to remain), or provide the alien with relief. In the case of an ordered deportation, an alien has 10 days to appeal to the Board of Immigration Appeals.

Aliens found deportable and who are not granted an appeal are returned to the country they chose at the beginning of the hearing. In the case of those returning to Mexico, Immigration and Customs Enforcement officers put deportees on chartered buses. In order to be certain the deportees do not immediately try to re-enter the United States, the buses drive well into Mexico before releasing the passengers, who sometimes may be hundreds of miles away from their homes.

Depending on the nature of their immigration violations, deported aliens are prohibited to enter the United States for a period of between 5 and 20 years. Only special permission from immigration authorities will allow them back into the United States before this period has ended.

8 ALTERNATIVES TO REMOVAL

Aliens facing deportation sometimes can pursue different alternatives through what is known as "discretionary relief." Both parties involved—the government and the alien—have reasons to consider this option. Some forms of relief save the government time and money; others aid aliens who are truly in need, or who face danger if they are returned to their homelands.

When aliens apply for discretionary relief, they admit to their deportability yet ask the judge to reconsider their removal anyway. As the name implies, discretionary relief is completely up to the "discretion" of the immigration judge. If an alien does not meet the qualifications for relief, the judge must not grant it. In the majority of cases, aliens have to make their request before or during the deportation hearing.

Voluntary Departure and Asylum

The most common type of discretionary relief is voluntary departure. By applying for this status, an alien is asking permission to leave the country on his or her own instead of being deported. Voluntary departure may be an attractive option for several reasons: it does not have the stigma or the legal consequences of deportation, and the alien can reapply to return to the United States, while deported aliens are kept from returning for 5 to 20 years.

◀Haitian Americans march the streets of Miami in November 2002, protesting the government's policy of detaining Haitian asylum seekers for an indefinite period. Receiving asylum is one of the better alternatives to deportation, though sometimes asylum seekers must go through a lengthy process to obtain it.

To receive voluntary departure, an alien must be able to pay for travel expenses out of the country. He or she must also demonstrate conduct of good moral character during the five years preceding the application. Immigration law leaves it up to the courts to interpret what "good moral character" is, although it provides examples of what it is not: People of good moral character do not perjure themselves for immigration benefits, or help other undocumented immigrants enter the country. They have not been convicted of any drug crimes, crimes of moral turpitude, or any two or more crimes with combined sentences of over five years.

Aliens granted voluntary departure are given a brief period—its exact length determined by a judge—to settle their affairs before leaving. Occasionally, the government awards extended forms of voluntary departure to select groups of people. In the past, these groups have included nationals from Afghanistan, Vietnam, Chile, Cuba, Iran, Nicaragua, and Poland—all countries that at various times were considered too dangerous for aliens to return to.

Other forms of discretionary relief do not require the alien to leave the country. One such type is cancellation of removal, which changes an immigrant's status from "undocumented" to "lawful permanent resident." In order to qualify for cancellation, an alien must have demonstrated conduct of good moral character, and have been continuously present in the United States for at least seven years.

Some aliens facing deportation request asylum. The application is completed either before a deportation order has been issued (affirmative application) or during deportation proceedings, after the alien has been taken into custody (defensive application). An alien is eligible for asylum if he or she fits the definition of a refugee—someone "unable or unwilling to return to his or her home country due to a fear of persecution." If immigration officers are convinced that an alien making an affirmative application deserves asylum, they can grant this form of relief. However, if they have doubts about

In 2000 U.S. Marine Jason Johnson (right) helped Meriam al-Khalifa (left), a member of the royal family of Bahrain, to flee her country and illegally enter the United States, where they were married in November. She applied to the U.S. government for asylum as a defense against deportation, testifying that her life was in danger if she was ordered to return to Bahrain.

the alien's asylum claim, they will refer the case to immigration court. For those aliens already in custody, the asylum decision rests solely with the immigration judge.

Aliens who have been longtime residents in the United States have their own options, which are offered by the "registry" provisions of immigration law. If an alien entered the country (either legally or illegally) before 1972, registry can change his or her status to "lawful permanent resident." With the passing of the Immigration Reform and Control Act of 1986, the original deadline of January 1, 1948, was moved up to January 1, 1972.

Some groups of undocumented immigrants are granted "deferred enforced departure," or DED. By granting aliens of a certain group or nationality this status, the government promises that it will not take steps to deport them. It is not a substitute for a green card, but it is an indication that the government will use discretion for aliens who fall within this category.

Estoppel and the Appeal Process

Deportations can also be *estopped*, a legal term for preventing something from happening. Estoppel takes place if the action that made an alien deportable was based on faulty advice that he or she received from a government employee.

A stay of deportation is like an estoppel, in that it halts the deportation order; however, it is only temporary. The district director of the BICE grants the stay, sometimes for the purpose of allotting more time for an alien's permanent resident application to be processed. More often, the stay gives aliens more time to appeal a court's decision and postpone the actual deportation until that appeal is resolved.

The appeal to a deportation order asks a judge or another legal body to reconsider a case. A case may need reconsideration because the hearing was conducted improperly or new evidence has been found. In some instances, a judge may have simply given an improper ruling.

There are three types of appeals to removal hearings, and each appeal stays the deportation order until it is resolved. The simplest appeal is called a motion to reopen or reconsider. If new evidence comes to light, an alien's counsel can move to reopen the case, which is decided by the immigration judge. Cases are rarely reopened, however. The new evidence that is presented is held to a very tight standard: it must be relevant to the case and not have been available at the time of the hearing. If the standard on the evidence were looser, immigration courts would be clogged with appeals, and judges would have to hear the same cases over and over.

The second type of appeal, the administrative appeal, is made to the Board of Immigration Appeals (BIA) instead of the original immigration judge. If the BIA decides the case has merit, it will hear the argument of the alien's counsel. The BIA can uphold or overturn removal orders, discretionary relief decisions, and even administrative fines. It can also send the case back to the immigration judge for reconsideration. On rare occasions, it will forward the case to the attorney general.

An alien's final appeal option is judicial review. The Court of Appeals will review an immigration judge's decision, but only in response to a petition of a final deportation order. The alien must still be in the United States when the petition is made, and it must take place within six months after the deportation order. In 1996, Congress placed limitations on the judicial review process when it passed the Illegal Immigration Reform and Immigrant Responsibility Act (IIRAIRA).

The Court of Appeals is only responsible for reviewing the hearing and how it was conducted, not the facts of the case itself, and only if the court decides that the hearing was conducted improperly will it reopen the case. When dealing with hearings in which it has found discrimination to have taken place, the Court of Appeals has the power to overturn the ruling.

9 DEPORTATION AFTER SEPTEMBER 11

On the morning of September 11, 2001, a group of terrorists launched a devastating attack on the United States, hijacking four passenger airliners and using them as weapons. In New York City, two of the planes crashed into the Twin Towers of the World Trade Center and killed thousands of people in a couple of hours. More people died in the other attacks, one of which crashed into a wing of the Pentagon in Washington, D.C.

In the days that followed, the nation dealt with the shock of this powerful blow delivered by a then-unknown enemy. The evidence pointed to an international terrorist organization called al-Qaeda, and President George W. Bush responded by declaring a war on terror to ferret out al-Qaeda and similar groups. Between late 2001 and 2003, the United States organized military campaigns in Afghanistan and Iraq, countries with known or suspected terrorist connections. However, much of the war was also fought at home through non-military means. While many actions have been applauded, others have been controversial.

The Controversy of the Detainees

In the months following September 11, the FBI and the Department of Justice sought to root out the terrorist network

◄ Smoke rises from the World Trade Center moments after two hijacked planes have crashed into its towers, September 11, 2001. As part of the investigation of the terrorist attacks, the Justice Department arrested and detained more than 1,000 undocumented immigrants.

behind the attacks that was operating within the country. More than 1,000 people were arrested and detained during the investigation. Much of what the public knows of their detention comes from a report issued in April 2003 by the Office of the Inspector General, entitled "The September 11 Detainees: A Review of the Treatment of Aliens Held on Immigration Charges in Connection with the Investigation of the September 11 Attacks." The FBI placed the detainees into three categories: "of high interest," "of interest," and "of undetermined interest." The majority of those classified "of high interest" were placed into custody at the Metropolitan Detention Center (MDC) in Brooklyn, New York. Most of the remaining detainees were held in the Passaic County Jail in Paterson, New Jersey.

Detainees at the MDC experienced harsh conditions. Prisoners were locked down for 23-hour stretches. Lights were constantly kept on in their cells, hindering their ability to sleep. When prisoners were moved they were shackled, and they had extremely limited access to their families and legal counsel. There were also reports of physical and verbal abuse, although none of them were substantiated enough for the detainees to press charges.

Inmates at Passaic faced better conditions. The prison had been under INS contract for the past 15 years, so the staff was at least experienced with this type of prisoner. Detainees had greater visiting and phone privileges, and though there were a few reports of verbal abuse, none were to the extent reported at the MDC.

Still, critics of the policy argued that the detainees should not have been held long as they were, or even held at all. They argued that the INS (at that point it was not yet reorganized) did not notify the detainees of their violations in a timely manner, which may have prevented many of them from obtaining the legal counsel to which they were entitled. And while some detainees were legitimate subjects of the FBI's investigation, others were people who simply were picked up for immigration

The private quarters and exercise area of a typical detention facility. Many deportable aliens receive bail to avoid detention; however, the suspects of the investigation following the September 2001 attacks faced extended detention periods while their cases were resolved.

violations. Were it not for the terrorist attacks, many of the violators would have been released on bond after they were given a deportation hearing date.

The detainees were not given a hearing at the proper date because the Justice Department had instituted a "hold until cleared" policy, which meant their case would not be heard until the FBI cleared them of suspicion. Government officials hoped that the policy would not only keep terrorist suspects from fleeing, but that it also would create gaps in the network and hinder future attacks. These clearances took much longer than originally expected, however. The average detainee took 80 days to clear, and one particular inmate's clearance came after 244 days. The Justice Department changed the policy in January 2002, lifting the requirement on the INS to wait for the FBI's review of the detainees.

During the period that the "hold until cleared" policy was in place, the INS was expected to take only 90 days after an alien's arrest to arrange for his or her deportation or release. However, in many cases the INS worked past the 90-day dead-line. Only 347 of the detainees were released within the first 100 days of the detention period, and only 174 more were released within the first 150 days. The rest waited even longer.

The Office of Legal Counsel (OLC), the legal advising arm of the Department of Justice, offered a justification of the delays in February 2003. Officials acknowledged that under typical circumstances, the INS was obligated to make a decision within 90 days; however, under these unusual circumstances the terrorist investigations took precedence and the law allowed for the delays.

There was also controversy surrounding the INS's review methods. Under regulation, detainees held longer than 90 days are entitled to a Post-Order Custody Review (POCR), a proce-dure that determines if the continued detention of an alien is warranted. The Office of the Inspector General (OIG) took a sample of 54 delayed-custody aliens and found that only 3 received a POCR, and at least one of these was conducted late.

In response to criticism of the investigation, Deputy Attorney General Larry D. Thompson publicly defended the government's actions. He argued that certainly no agency in the United States had ever dealt with an attack of the magnitude of September 11 before. He wrote that the mission was part of a wider effort to prevent further acts of terrorism, and "the detention of those illegal aliens suspected of involvement with terrorism was paramount to that mission." It would be "unfair," he argued, to criticize his staff for implementing the policies under these circumstances.

Special Registration

In November 2002, the government continued its crackdown by calling for aliens from 25 countries—24 of which were predominantly Muslim—to take part in Special Registration. The registration required that any male over 16 years old who was living temporarily in the United States (also known as a "non-immigrant") was given a deadline to report to the INS. U.S. citizens and nationals, lawful permanent residents, asylum seekers, and diplomats did not need to register.

During the Special Registration, agents interviewed all available subjects, asking about their jobs and how they made their income. Each alien was also photographed, fingerprinted, and received criminal background checks. Most aliens were soon released, and those who had violated the terms of their admissions were scheduled for removal hearings.

This program also proved to be controversial. While the Justice Department claimed it was part of its strategy to deter terrorism, critics pointed out that terrorists or criminals would either not register or would lie during the interviews. They stated that terrorists would not have their plans thwarted simply because an official with no intelligence information on them sought an interview. The criticism proved to be legitimate, as some aliens simply decided not to register, and those who did were generally either in compliance with the law or only guilty of minor violations.

As another part of the government's efforts, more resources and attention were given to student visa violators. Since 1996, Congress had ordered the INS to develop an electronic student-tracking system; however, it was only after the September 11 attacks that Congress appropriated the money to make the program a reality. SEVIS (Student and Exchange Visitor Information System) keeps track of the personal, academic, and disciplinary records of foreign students across the country. The INS compiles records from the information sent by more than 4,000 participating schools and universities. Those schools that did not participate were no longer allowed to enroll foreign students.

Students were investigated if their course load dropped below the required number of credits needed to maintain foreign-student status. Some students with visas never showed up for school at all. BICE special agents were responsible for tracking these students down.

A student services director at American University in Washington, D.C., demonstrates the new Student and Exchange Visitor Information System (SEVIS) on a laptop computer. The system, first developed by the INS, is designed to keep up-to-date records of foreign students across the country and identify those students violating their visas.

Deportation, and the special investigations that locate deportable aliens, help ensure that U.S. immigration laws are being observed. However, the deportation process must proceed fairly and without discrimination. Decisions to remove residents and guests of the country must not be taken lightly. When immigration courts and officials act with great care, removing people only as justice and good sense dictate, deserving immigrants entering the country can still expect to find opportunities and basic freedoms.

CHRONOLOGY

1882 The United States passes its first immigration laws, designed to exclude Chinese workers, as well as convicts, the mentally insane, and others.

1921 The Immigration Act of 1921 initiates the national-origins quota system.

1924 The Immigration Act of 1924 makes the national-origins quotas permanent and establishes the Border Patrol.

1933 The Immigration Service merges with the Naturalization Bureau to form the Immigration and Naturalization Service (INS).

1942 The United States and Mexico initiate the bracero program, which permits millions of Mexican agricultural workers to work temporarily in the United States.

1954 Operation Wetback removes many Mexican immigrants from Texas but is also unpopular.

1965 The Immigration Act of 1965 is signed, ending the national-origins quota system.

1986 The Immigration Reform and Control Act makes it unlawful for an employer to knowingly hire undocumented immigrants.

1993 Operation Hold the Line begins in El Paso, Texas; the *Golden Venture* runs aground in New York City, killing 10 smuggled Chinese nationals.

1994   Operation Gatekeeper begins in San Diego.

1996   Congress passes the Illegal Immigration Reform
        and Immigrant Responsibility Act (IIRIRA),
        expanding the grounds of deportability and
        making it more difficult for longtime undocumented
        immigrants to stay in the country.

2001   Terrorists attack the World Trade Center and the
        Pentagon on September 11; the FBI and the
        Department of Justice initiates an investigation in
        which it arrests and detains more than 1,000
        people deemed to be national security risks.

2003   The Department of Homeland Security replaces
        the INS and delegates the service's former duties
        to the BCIS, BICE, and other departments.

GLOSSARY

absconder—an alien who flees instead of reporting to his or her deportation hearing.

appeal—a motion to reconsider a legal case.

asylee—an alien in the United States who receives asylum, meeting the legal definition of an individual who is unable or unwilling to return to his or her home country due to a fear of persecution.

cancellation of removal—a form of discretionary relief in which an alien is granted lawful permanent resident status.

coyote—a name for those who smuggle undocumented immigrants across the Mexican border.

deportation—the formal removal of an alien by the government after he or she has broken immigration laws.

discretionary relief—a ruling by an immigration judge that sets aside deportation due to special circumstances.

estoppel—a legal prevention of an action; in immigration terms, a halt to a deportation.

exclusion—the denial of an alien seeking to enter a country.

expedited removal—the immediate removal from the United States of an alien at a port of entry.

lawful permanent resident—a noncitizen legally residing in the United States.

moral turpitude—a designation of a kind of immorality used in determining an alien's deportability.

national—a citizen of a particular nation.

naturalization—the process of becoming a citizen.

parole—the process in which an inspector or other official allows aliens to enter the United States but without a guarantee that they will stay indefinitely.

pollo—an undocumented immigrant smuggled across the Mexican border by a coyote; literally, "chicken" in Spanish.

quota—a legal limit on the number of immigrants, usually within specific categories of region or country.

refugee—a person who is unable or unwilling to return to his or her home country because of persecution or a well-founded fear of persecution.

snakehead—a name for criminals who smuggle undocumented immigrants into the United States.

subpoena—a legal order to compel testimony from an unwilling witness.

subversive—a person who enters the United States to undermine or overthrow its government or other institutions.

visa—an official authorization that allows a person to enter the country at a port.

voluntary departure—a form of discretionary relief in which an alien may leave the United States without being deported.

withholding of removal—a form of discretionary relief in which an alien is allowed to remain in the country due to a fear of danger in his or her own homeland.

FURTHER READING

Andreas, Peter. *Border Games*. Ithaca, N.Y.: Cornell University Press, 2000.

Capaldi, Nicholas, ed. *Immigration: Debating the Issues*. Amherst, N.Y.: Prometheus Books, 1997.

Castles, Stephen, and Mark J. Miller. *The Age of Migration*, 2nd ed. New York: The Guilford Press, 1998.

Conover, Ted. *Coyotes*. New York: Vintage Books, 1987.

Cothran, Helen, ed. *Illegal Immigration*. San Diego, Calif.: Greenhaven Press, 2001.

Gonzalez-Pando, Miguel. *The Cuban Americans*. Westport, Conn.: Greenwood Press, 1998.

Hauser, Pierre N. *Illegal Aliens*. New York: Chelsea House Publishers, 1990.

Isbister, John. *The Immigration Debate: Remaking America*. West Hartford, Conn.: Kumarian Press, 1996.

LeDuff, Charlie. "A Wanderer for Peace Has Run Out of Road," *The New York Times*, Feb. 1, 2003.

Lee, Kathleen. *Illegal Immigration*. San Diego, Calif.: Lucent Books, 1996.

Loescher, Gil, and John A. Scanlan. *Calculated Kindness*. New York: The Free Press, 1986.

Poynter, Margaret. *The Uncertain Journey*. New York: Maxwell Macmillan International, 1992.

Wambaugh, Joseph. *Lines and Shadows*. New York: William Morrow and Company, 1984.

FURTHER READING

Weissbrodt, David. *Immigration Law and Procedure In a Nutshell*. Saint Paul, Minn.: West Publishing Company, 1989.

Zucker, Norman L., and Naomi Flink Zucker. *Desperate Crossings: Seeking Refuge in America*. Armonk, N.Y: M.E. Sharpe, 1996.

INTERNET RESOURCES

http://www.bcis.gov

The website of the Bureau of Citizenship and Immigration services explains the various functions of the organization and provides specific information on immigration policy.

http://www.canadianhistory.ca/iv/main.html

This site contains an excellent history of immigration to Canada from the 1800s to the present.

http://www.customs.gov

The homepage of the Bureau of Customs and Border Protection, an agency of the Department of Homeland Security, keeps the public informed about travel and import/export guidelines.

http://www.bice.immigration.gov

This site is an informative source covering the operations of the Bureau of Immigration and Customs Enforcement, part of the Department of Homeland Security.

http://www.dhs.gov

The official site of the Department of Homeland Security covers in detail the multifaceted agenda of this newly formed branch.

http://www.aila.org

The homepage of the American Immigration Lawyers Association is a resource for advocates of fair immigration policy and for immigrants in need of legal counsel.

INTERNET RESOURCES

http://www.lchr.org

The home site of the Lawyers Committee for Human Rights is an informative source, covering the organization's efforts to support refugees and other victims of persecution or repression.

http://www.immigration.gov/graphics/shared/lawenfor/ bpatrol

The homepage of the U.S. Border Patrol gives an overview of its operations, provides information on the border's sections, and has a link to media coverage of border activity and related issues.

INDEX

Numbers in **bold italic** refer to captions.

INDEX

CONTRIBUTORS

SENATOR EDWARD M. KENNEDY has represented Massachusetts in the United States Senate for more than forty years. Kennedy serves on the Senate Judiciary Committee, where he is the senior Democrat on the Immigration Subcommittee. He currently is the ranking member on the Health, Education, Labor and Pensions Committee in the Senate, and also serves on the Armed Services Committee, where he is a member of the Senate Arms Control Observer Group. He is also a member of the Congressional Friends of Ireland and a trustee of the John F. Kennedy Center for the Performing Arts in Washington, D.C.

Throughout his career, Kennedy has fought for issues that benefit the citizens of Massachusetts and the nation, including the effort to bring quality health care to every American, education reform, raising the minimum wage, defending the rights of workers and their families, strengthening the civil rights laws, assisting individuals with disabilities, fighting for cleaner water and cleaner air, and protecting and strengthening Social Security and Medicare for senior citizens.

Kennedy is the youngest of nine children of Joseph P. and Rose Fitzgerald Kennedy, and is a graduate of Harvard University and the University of Virginia Law School. His home is in Hyannis Port, Massachusetts, where he lives with his wife, Victoria Reggie Kennedy, and children, Curran and Caroline. He also has three grown children, Kara, Edward Jr., and Patrick, and four grandchildren.

Senior consulting editor STUART ANDERSON served as Executive Associate Commissioner for Policy and Planning and Counselor to the Commissioner at the Immigration and Naturalization Service from August 2001 until January 2003. He spent four and a half years on Capitol Hill on the Senate Immigration Subcommittee, first for Senator Spencer Abraham and then as Staff Director of the subcommittee for Senator Sam Brownback. Prior to that, he was Director of Trade and Immigration Studies at the Cato Institute in Washington, D.C., where he produced reports on the history of immigrants in the military and the role of immigrants in high technology. He currently serves as Executive Director of the National Foundation for American Policy, a nonpartisan public policy research organization focused on trade, immigration, and international relations. He has an M.A. from Georgetown University and a B.A. in Political Science from Drew University. His articles have appeared in such publications as the *Wall Street Journal*, *New York Times*, and *Los Angeles Times*.

MARIAN L. SMITH served as the senior historian of the U.S. Immigration and Naturalization Service (INS) from 1988 to 2003, and is currently the immigration and naturalization historian within the Department of Homeland Security in Washington, D.C. She studies, publishes, and speaks on the history of the immigration agency and is active in management of official 20th-century immigration records.

PETER HAMMERSCHMIDT is the First Secretary (Financial and Military Affairs) for the Permanent Mission of Canada to the United Nations. Before taking this position, he was a ministerial speechwriter and policy specialist for the Department of National

Defence in Ottawa. Prior to joining the public service, he served as the Publications Director for the Canadian Institute of Strategic Studies in Toronto. He has a B.A. (Honours) in Political Studies from Queen's University, and an MScEcon in Strategic Studies from the University of Wales, Aberystwyth. He currently lives in New York, where in his spare time he operates a freelance editing and writing service, Wordschmidt Communications.

Manuscript reviewer ESTHER OLAVARRIA serves as General Counsel to Senator Edward M. Kennedy, ranking Democrat on the U.S. Senate Judiciary Committee, Subcommittee on Immigration. She is Senator Kennedy's primary advisor on immigration, nationality, and refugee legislation and policies. Prior to her current job, she practiced immigration law in Miami, Florida, working at several non-profit organizations. She cofounded the Florida Immigrant Advocacy Center and served as managing attorney, supervising the direct service work of the organization and assisting in the advocacy work. She also worked at Legal Services of Greater Miami, as the directing attorney of the American Immigration Lawyers Association Pro Bono Project, and at the Haitian Refugee Center, as a staff attorney. She clerked for a Florida state appellate court after graduating from the University of Florida Law School. She was born in Havana, Cuba, and raised in Florida.

Reviewer JANICE V. KAGUYUTAN is Senator Edward M. Kennedy's advisor on immigration, nationality, and refugee legislation and policies. Prior to working on Capitol Hill, Ms. Kaguyutan was a staff attorney at the NOW Legal Defense and Education Fund's Immigrant Women Program. Ms. Kaguyutan has written and trained extensively on the rights of immigrant victims of domestic violence, sexual assault, and human trafficking. Her previous work includes representing battered immigrant women in civil protection order, child support, divorce, and custody hearings, as well as representing immigrants before the Immigration and Naturalization Service on a variety of immigration matters.

ROB STAEGER lives and writes in New Jersey. He has written dozens of short stories for children, and even more newspaper stories for adults. He has also written 10 books, including *Wyatt Earp*, *Native American Tools and Weapons*, and *The Journey of Lewis and Clark*. He would like to dedicate this book to his nephew Daniel, one of America's newest cute little bald citizens.

PICTURE CREDITS